RETURN OF THE DRAGON KING

PART 1: ALL'S FAIRY IN LOVE AND WAR

Written by:
RON MARZ and **DAVID A. RODRIGUEZ**

Art by:
FICO OSSIO

Colors by:
DAVID GARCIA CRUZ

Letters by:
DERON BENNETT

ABDO Spotlight

IDW

ABDOPUBLISHING.COM

Reinforced library bound edition published in 2019 by Spotlight, a division of ABDO
PO Box 398166, Minneapolis, Minnesota 55439. Spotlight produces high-quality
reinforced library bound editions for schools and libraries.
Published by agreement with IDW.

Printed in the United States of America, North Mankato, Minnesota.
042018
092018

THIS BOOK CONTAINS
RECYCLED MATERIALS

Originally published as SKYLANDERS issue #7.

Library of Congress Control Number: 2017961398

Publisher's Cataloging in Publication Data

Names: Marz, Ron, author. Rodriguez, David A., author. | Ossio, Fico; Cruz, David Garcia; Baldeón, David, illustrators.
Title: Return of the dragon king / writers: Ron Marz and David A. Rodriguez; art: Fico Ossio; David Garcia Cruz; David Baldeón.
Description: Reinforced library bound edition. | Minneapolis, MN : Spotlight, 2019 | Series: Skylanders set 2 | Part 1: All's fairy in love and war written by Ron Marz and David A. Rodriguez; illustrated by Fico Ossio and David Garcia Cruz. | Part 2: The menace of Malefor written by Ron Marz and David A. Rodriguez; illustrated by Fico Ossio and David Garcia Cruz. | Part 3: Reach for the sky written by Ron Marz and David A. Rodriguez; illustrated by Fico Ossio, David Baldeón & David Garcia Cruz.
Summary: Join your favorite Skylanders heroes in these all-new comic book adventures! Spyro, Cynder, and Hex discover their powers were stolen by a mysterious fairy to revive a malevolent and powerful enemy.
Identifiers: ISBN 9781532142468 (Part 1: All's fairy in love and war) | ISBN 9781532142475 (Part 2: The menace of Malefor) | ISBN 9781532142482 (Part 3: Reach for the sky)
Subjects: LCSH: Skylanders (Game)--Juvenile fiction. | Monsters--Juvenile fiction. | Rescues--Juvenile fiction. | Dragon--Juvenile fiction. | Race--Juvenile fiction. | Escapes--Juvenile fiction. | Imaginary wars and battles--Juvenile fiction. | Comic books, strips, etc.--Juvenile fiction.
Classification: DDC 741.5--dc23

ABDO
Spotlight

A Division of ABDO
abdopublishing.com

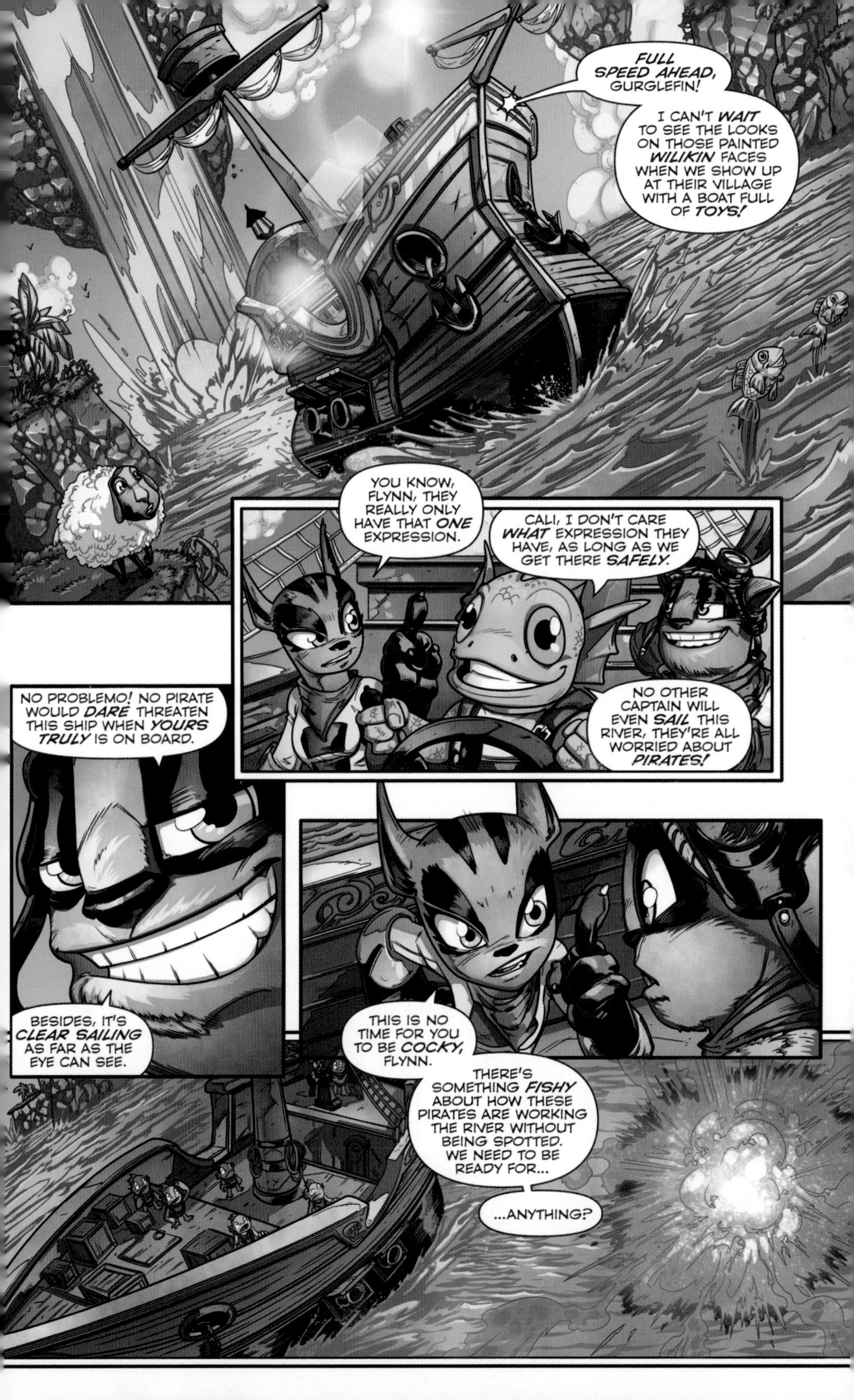
FULL SPEED AHEAD, GURGLEFIN!
I CAN'T WAIT TO SEE THE LOOKS ON THOSE PAINTED WILIKIN FACES WHEN WE SHOW UP AT THEIR VILLAGE WITH A BOAT FULL OF TOYS!
YOU KNOW, FLYNN, THEY REALLY ONLY HAVE THAT ONE EXPRESSION.
CALI, I DON'T CARE WHAT EXPRESSION THEY HAVE, AS LONG AS WE GET THERE SAFELY.
NO OTHER CAPTAIN WILL EVEN SAIL THIS RIVER, THEY'RE ALL WORRIED ABOUT PIRATES!
NO PROBLEMO! NO PIRATE WOULD DARE THREATEN THIS SHIP WHEN YOURS TRULY IS ON BOARD.
BESIDES, IT'S CLEAR SAILING AS FAR AS THE EYE CAN SEE.
THIS IS NO TIME FOR YOU TO BE COCKY, FLYNN.
THERE'S SOMETHING FISHY ABOUT HOW THESE PIRATES ARE WORKING THE RIVER WITHOUT BEING SPOTTED. WE NEED TO BE READY FOR...
...ANYTHING?

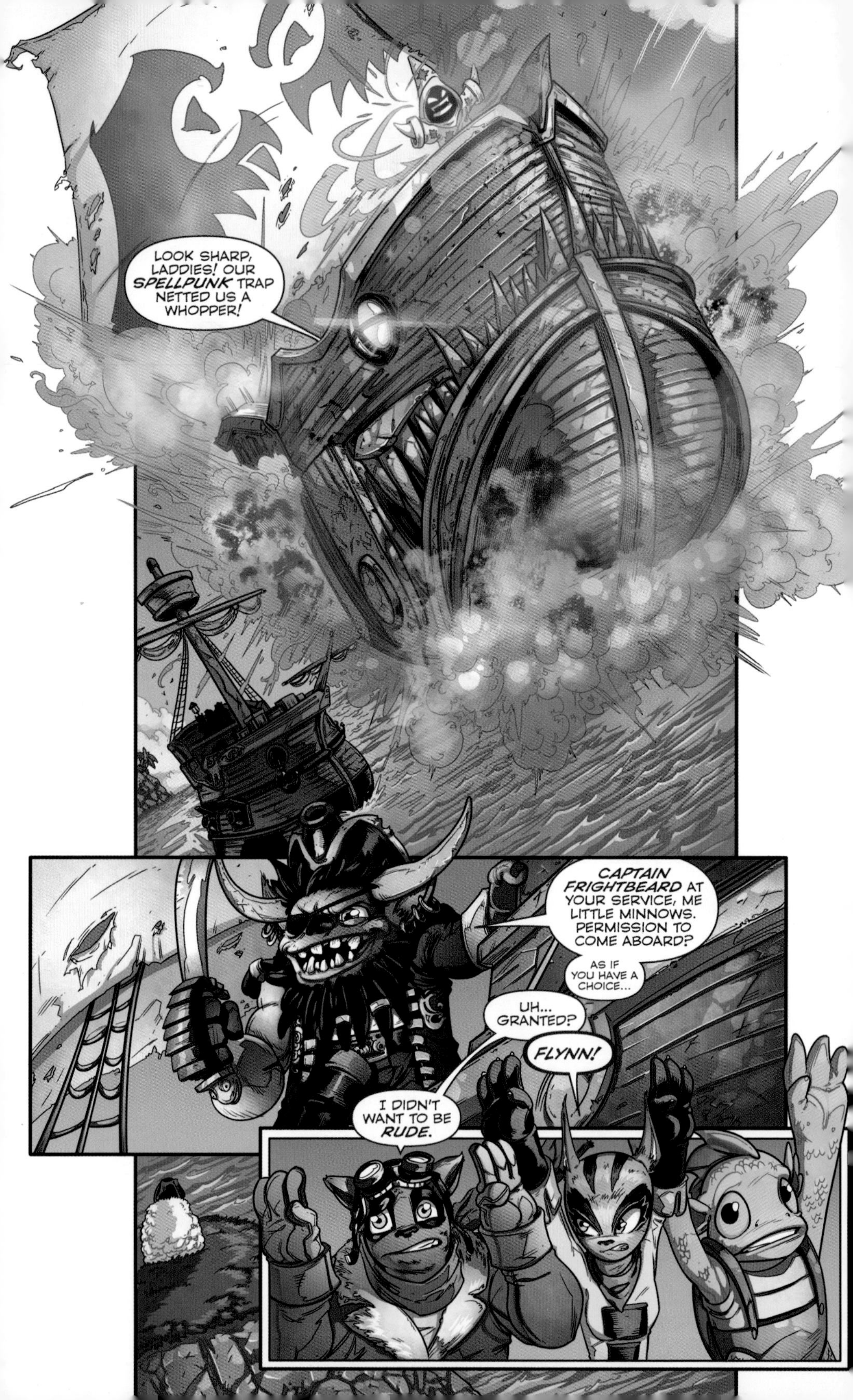
LOOK SHARP, LADDIES! OUR *SPELLPUNK* TRAP NETTED US A WHOPPER!
CAPTAIN FRIGHTBEARD AT YOUR SERVICE, ME LITTLE MINNOWS. PERMISSION TO COME ABOARD?
AS IF YOU HAVE A CHOICE...
UH... GRANTED?
FLYNN!
I DIDN'T WANT TO BE *RUDE*.

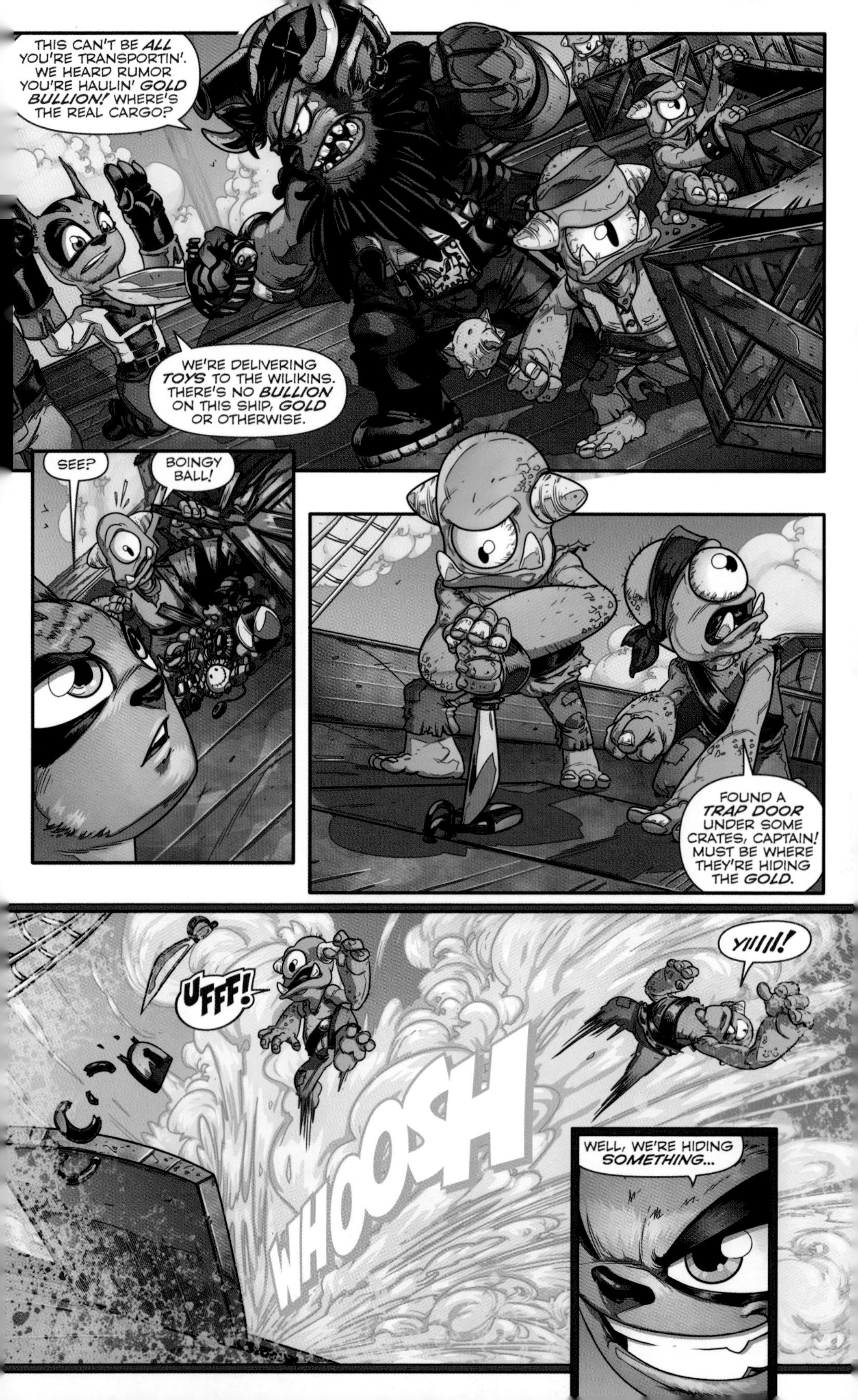
THIS CAN'T BE ALL YOU'RE TRANSPORTIN'. WE HEARD RUMOR YOU'RE HAULIN' GOLD BULLION! WHERE'S THE REAL CARGO?
WE'RE DELIVERING TOYS TO THE WILIKINS. THERE'S NO BULLION ON THIS SHIP, GOLD OR OTHERWISE.
SEE?
BOINGY BALL!
FOUND A TRAP DOOR UNDER SOME CRATES, CAPTAIN! MUST BE WHERE THEY'RE HIDING THE GOLD.
UFFF!
YIIIII!
WHOOSH
WELL, WE'RE HIDING SOMETHING...

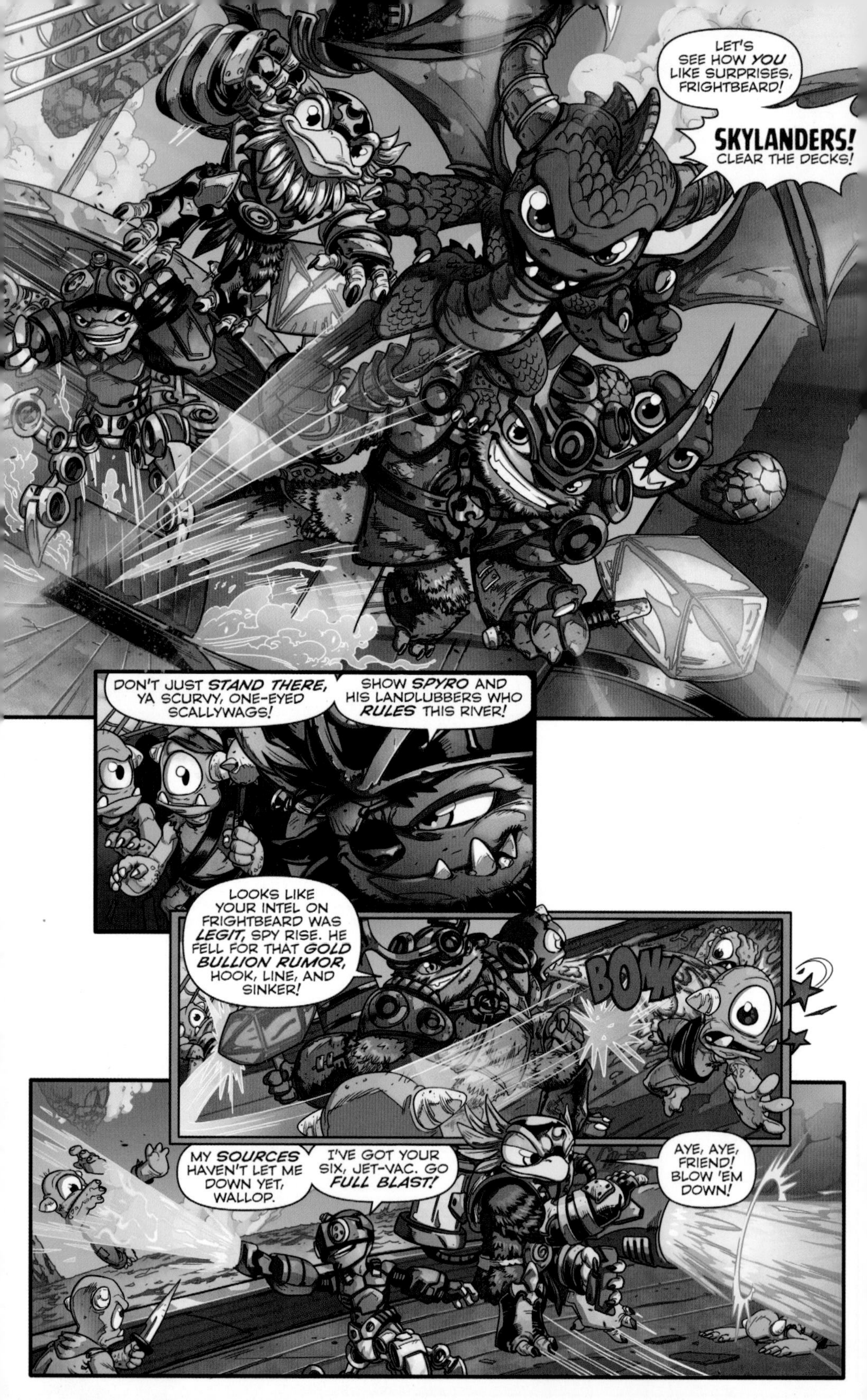
LET'S SEE HOW YOU LIKE SURPRISES, FRIGHTBEARD!
SKYLANDERS! CLEAR THE DECKS!
DON'T JUST STAND THERE, YA SCURVY, ONE-EYED SCALLYWAGS!
SHOW SPYRO AND HIS LANDLUBBERS WHO RULES THIS RIVER!
LOOKS LIKE YOUR INTEL ON FRIGHTBEARD WAS LEGIT, SPY RISE. HE FELL FOR THAT GOLD BULLION RUMOR, HOOK, LINE, AND SINKER!
BOW
MY SOURCES HAVEN'T LET ME DOWN YET, WALLOP.
I'VE GOT YOUR SIX, JET-VAC. GO FULL BLAST!
AYE, AYE, FRIEND! BLOW 'EM DOWN!

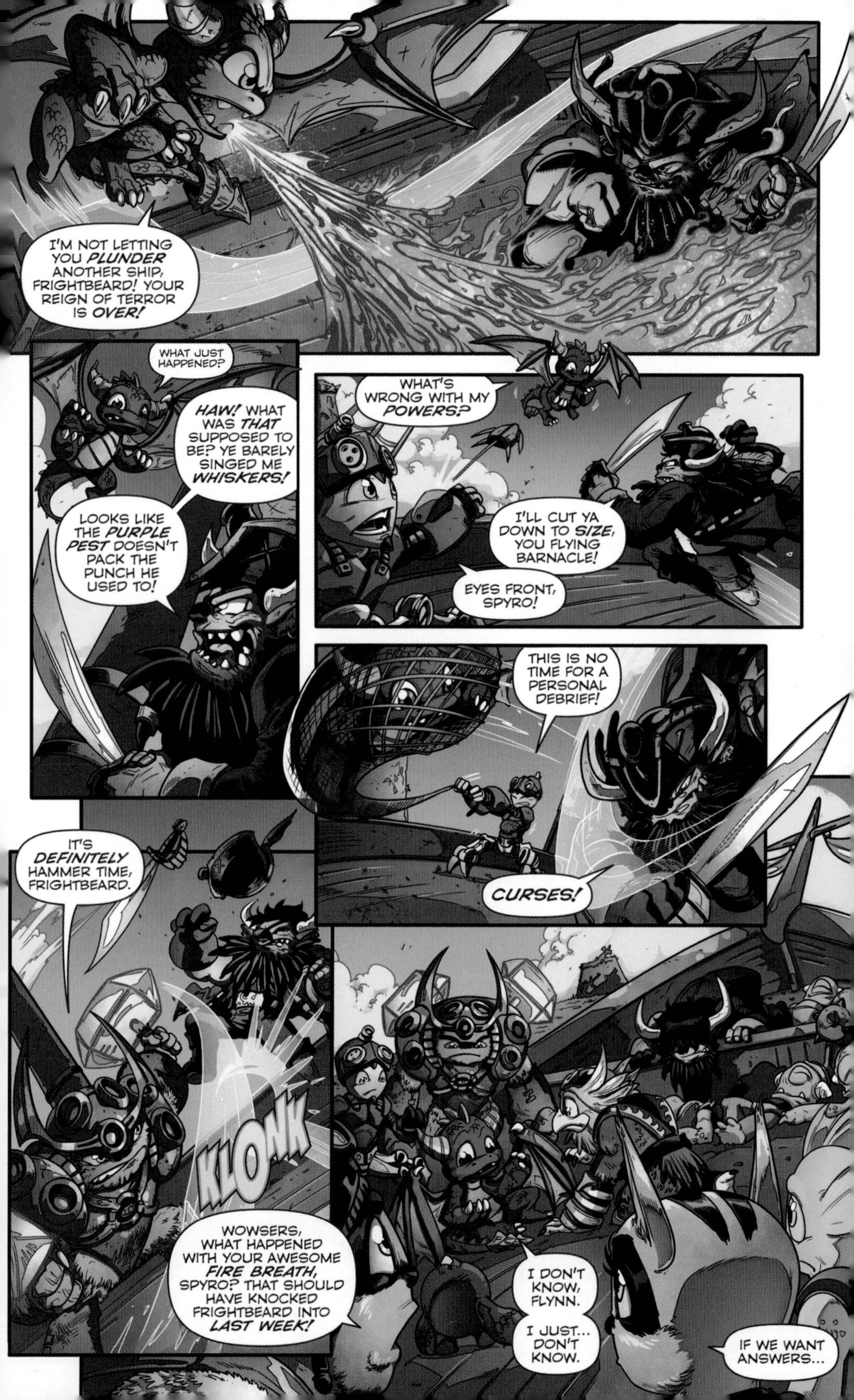
I'M NOT LETTING YOU PLUNDER ANOTHER SHIP, FRIGHTBEARD! YOUR REIGN OF TERROR IS OVER!
WHAT JUST HAPPENED?
HAW! WHAT WAS THAT SUPPOSED TO BE? YE BARELY SINGED ME WHISKERS!
LOOKS LIKE THE PURPLE PEST DOESN'T PACK THE PUNCH HE USED TO!
WHAT'S WRONG WITH MY POWERS?
I'LL CUT YA DOWN TO SIZE, YOU FLYING BARNACLE!
EYES FRONT, SPYRO!
THIS IS NO TIME FOR A PERSONAL DEBRIEF!
CURSES!
IT'S DEFINITELY HAMMER TIME, FRIGHTBEARD.
KLONK
WOWSERS, WHAT HAPPENED WITH YOUR AWESOME FIRE BREATH, SPYRO? THAT SHOULD HAVE KNOCKED FRIGHTBEARD INTO LAST WEEK!
I DON'T KNOW, FLYNN.
I JUST... DON'T KNOW.
IF WE WANT ANSWERS...

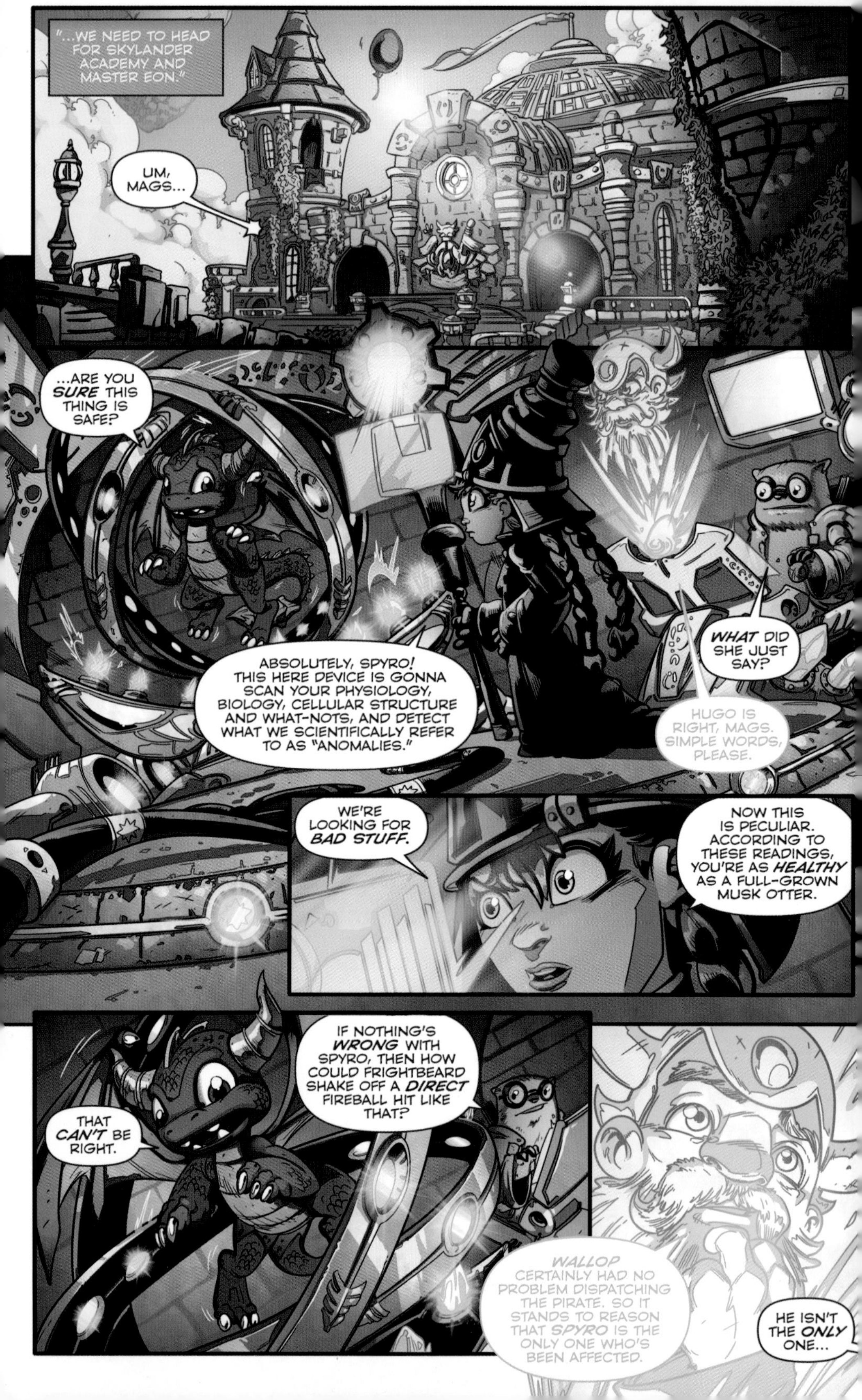

"...WE NEED TO HEAD FOR SKYLANDER ACADEMY AND MASTER EON."
UM, MAGS...
...ARE YOU SURE THIS THING IS SAFE?
ABSOLUTELY, SPYRO! THIS HERE DEVICE IS GONNA SCAN YOUR PHYSIOLOGY, BIOLOGY, CELLULAR STRUCTURE AND WHAT-NOTS, AND DETECT WHAT WE SCIENTIFICALLY REFER TO AS "ANOMALIES."
WHAT DID SHE JUST SAY?
HUGO IS RIGHT, MAGS. SIMPLE WORDS, PLEASE.
WE'RE LOOKING FOR BAD STUFF.
NOW THIS IS PECULIAR. ACCORDING TO THESE READINGS, YOU'RE AS HEALTHY AS A FULL-GROWN MUSK OTTER.
THAT CAN'T BE RIGHT.
IF NOTHING'S WRONG WITH SPYRO, THEN HOW COULD FRIGHTBEARD SHAKE OFF A DIRECT FIREBALL HIT LIKE THAT?
WALLOP CERTAINLY HAD NO PROBLEM DISPATCHING THE PIRATE. SO IT STANDS TO REASON THAT SPYRO IS THE ONLY ONE WHO'S BEEN AFFECTED.
HE ISN'T THE ONLY ONE...

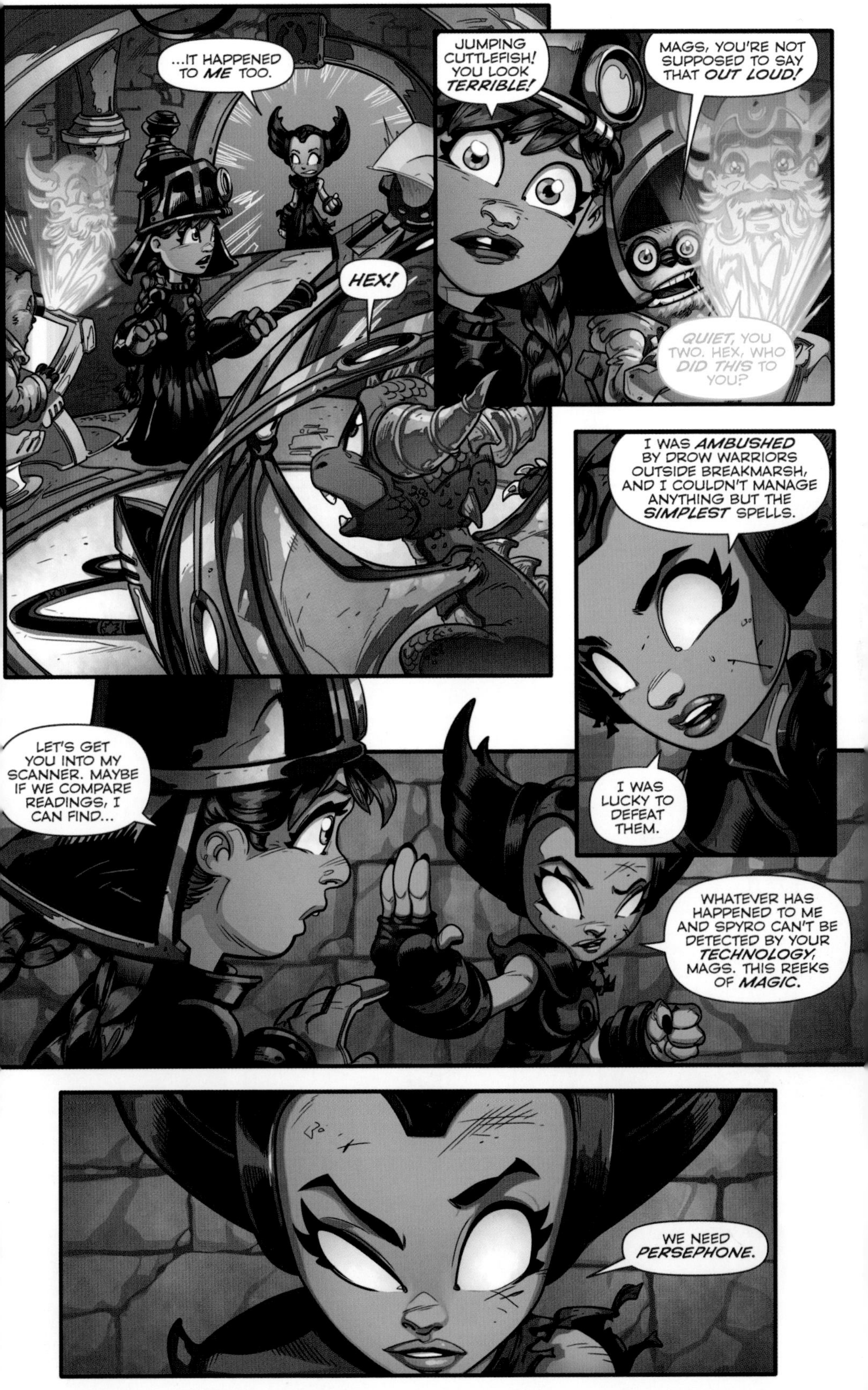

...IT HAPPENED TO ME TOO.
HEX!
JUMPING CUTTLEFISH! YOU LOOK TERRIBLE!
MAGS, YOU'RE NOT SUPPOSED TO SAY THAT OUT LOUD!
QUIET, YOU TWO. HEX, WHO DID THIS TO YOU?
I WAS AMBUSHED BY DROW WARRIORS OUTSIDE BREAKMARSH, AND I COULDN'T MANAGE ANYTHING BUT THE SIMPLEST SPELLS.
I WAS LUCKY TO DEFEAT THEM.
LET'S GET YOU INTO MY SCANNER. MAYBE IF WE COMPARE READINGS, I CAN FIND...
WHATEVER HAS HAPPENED TO ME AND SPYRO CAN'T BE DETECTED BY YOUR TECHNOLOGY, MAGS. THIS REEKS OF MAGIC.
WE NEED PERSEPHONE.

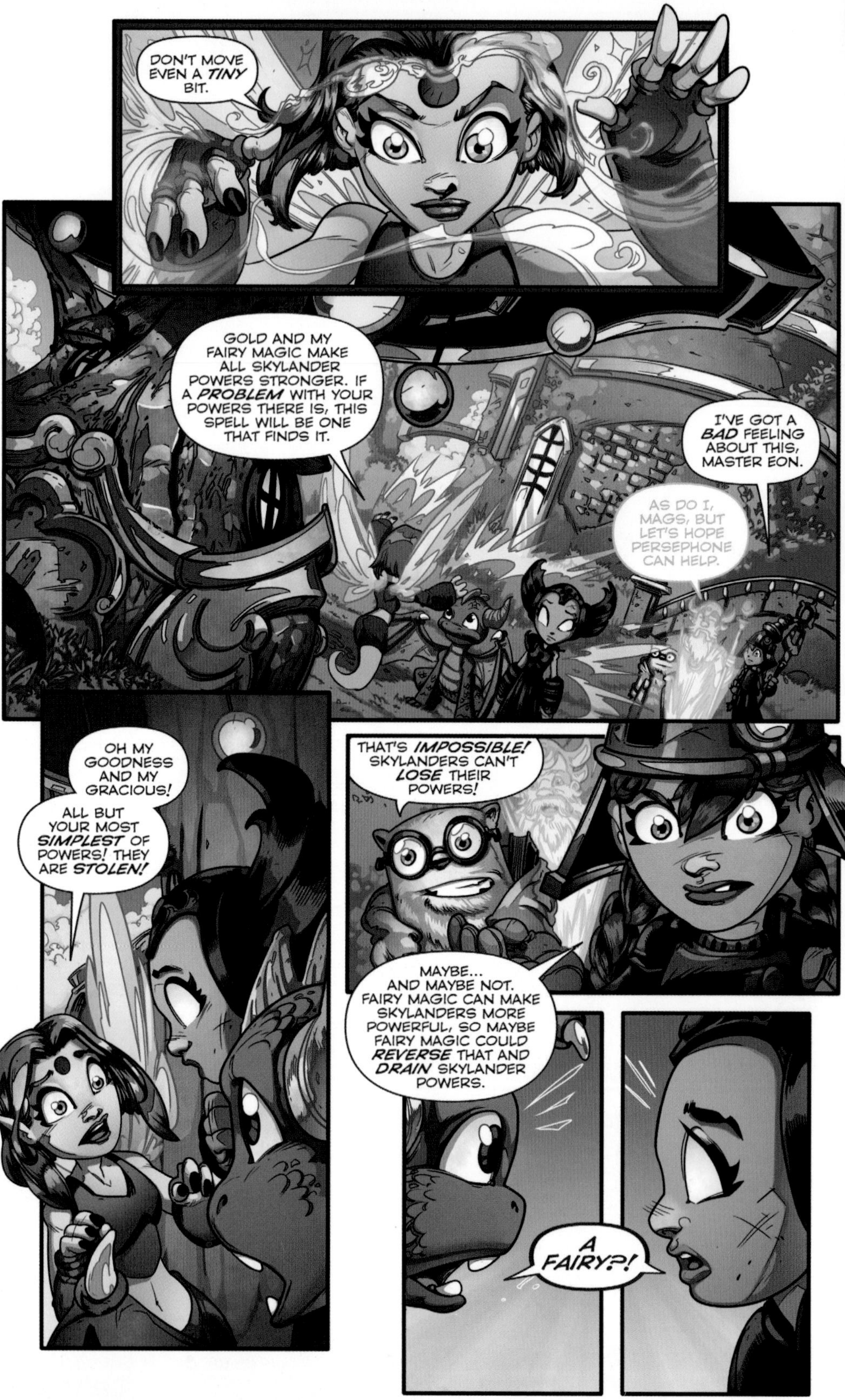

DON'T MOVE EVEN A TINY BIT.
GOLD AND MY FAIRY MAGIC MAKE ALL SKYLANDER POWERS STRONGER. IF A PROBLEM WITH YOUR POWERS THERE IS, THIS SPELL WILL BE ONE THAT FINDS IT.
I'VE GOT A BAD FEELING ABOUT THIS, MASTER EON.
AS DO I, MAGS, BUT LET'S HOPE PERSEPHONE CAN HELP.
OH MY GOODNESS AND MY GRACIOUS!
ALL BUT YOUR MOST SIMPLEST OF POWERS! THEY ARE STOLEN!
THAT'S IMPOSSIBLE! SKYLANDERS CAN'T LOSE THEIR POWERS!
MAYBE... AND MAYBE NOT. FAIRY MAGIC CAN MAKE SKYLANDERS MORE POWERFUL, SO MAYBE FAIRY MAGIC COULD REVERSE THAT AND DRAIN SKYLANDER POWERS.
A FAIRY?!

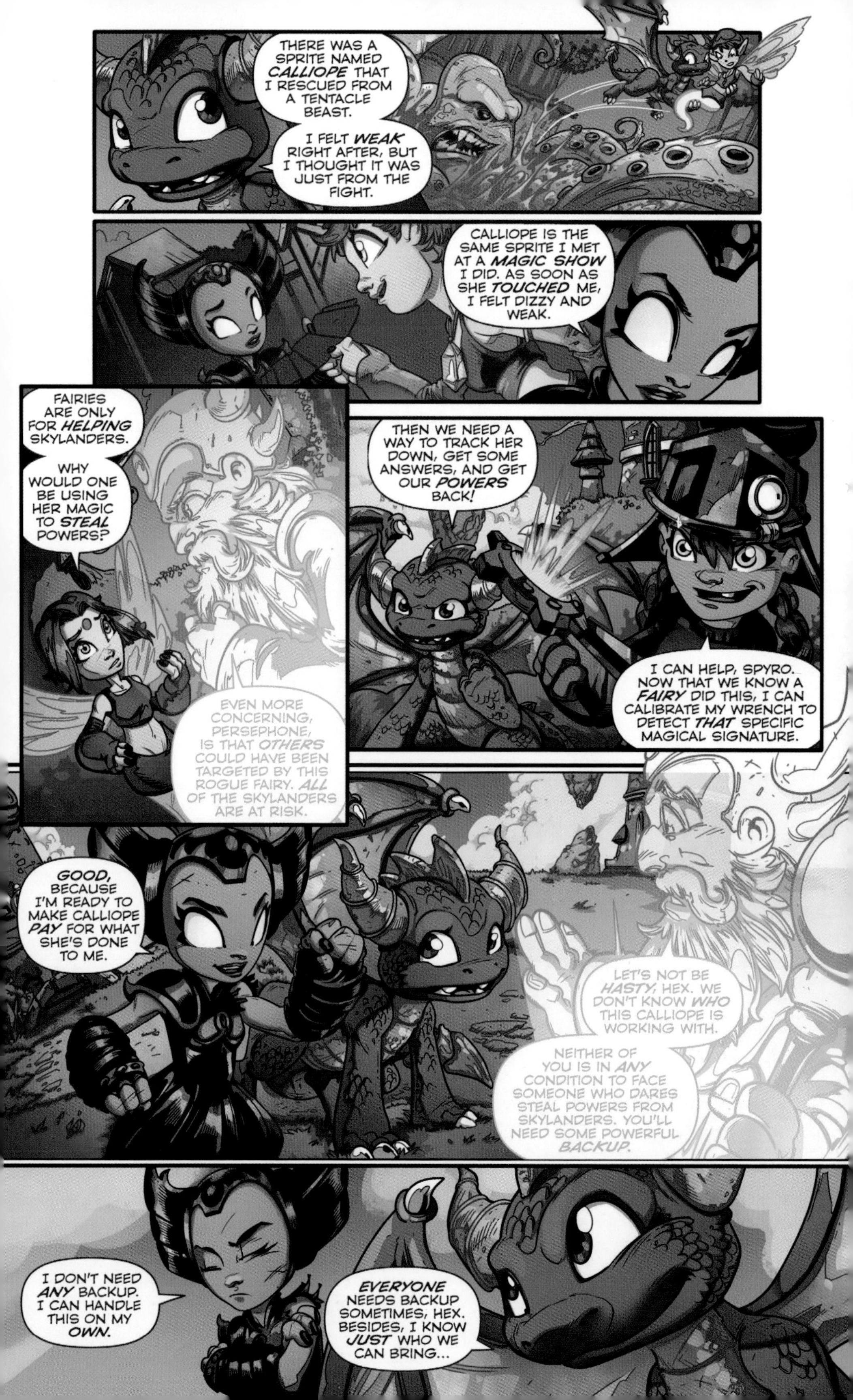
THERE WAS A SPRITE NAMED CALLIOPE THAT I RESCUED FROM A TENTACLE BEAST.
I FELT WEAK RIGHT AFTER, BUT I THOUGHT IT WAS JUST FROM THE FIGHT.
CALLIOPE IS THE SAME SPRITE I MET AT A MAGIC SHOW I DID. AS SOON AS SHE TOUCHED ME, I FELT DIZZY AND WEAK.
FAIRIES ARE ONLY FOR HELPING SKYLANDERS.
WHY WOULD ONE BE USING HER MAGIC TO STEAL POWERS?
EVEN MORE CONCERNING, PERSEPHONE, IS THAT OTHERS COULD HAVE BEEN TARGETED BY THIS ROGUE FAIRY. ALL OF THE SKYLANDERS ARE AT RISK.
THEN WE NEED A WAY TO TRACK HER DOWN, GET SOME ANSWERS, AND GET OUR POWERS BACK!
I CAN HELP, SPYRO. NOW THAT WE KNOW A FAIRY DID THIS, I CAN CALIBRATE MY WRENCH TO DETECT THAT SPECIFIC MAGICAL SIGNATURE.
GOOD, BECAUSE I'M READY TO MAKE CALLIOPE PAY FOR WHAT SHE'S DONE TO ME.
LET'S NOT BE HASTY, HEX. WE DON'T KNOW WHO THIS CALLIOPE IS WORKING WITH.
NEITHER OF YOU IS IN ANY CONDITION TO FACE SOMEONE WHO DARES STEAL POWERS FROM SKYLANDERS. YOU'LL NEED SOME POWERFUL BACKUP.
I DON'T NEED ANY BACKUP. I CAN HANDLE THIS ON MY OWN.
EVERYONE NEEDS BACKUP SOMETIMES, HEX. BESIDES, I KNOW JUST WHO WE CAN BRING...

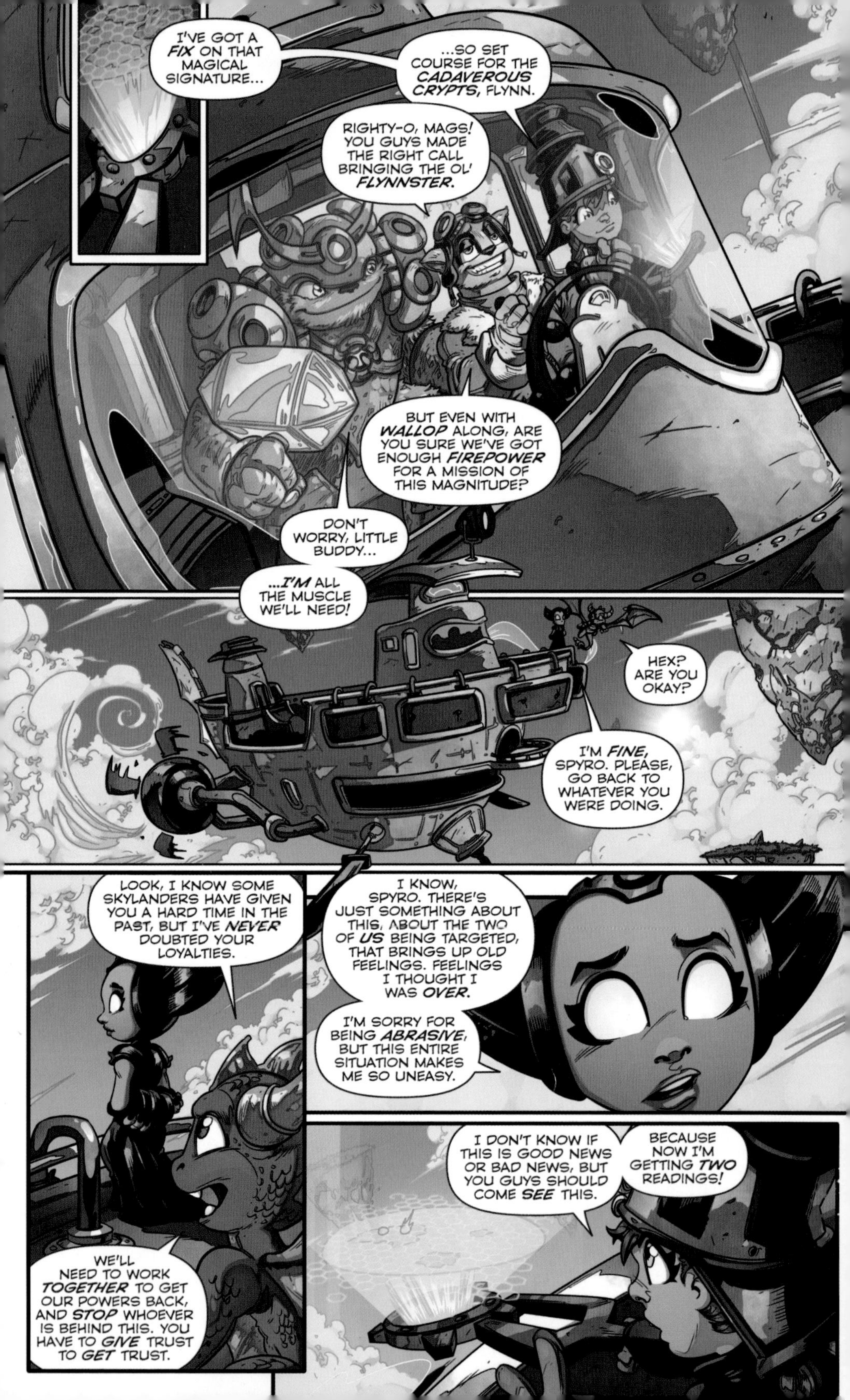
I'VE GOT A FIX ON THAT MAGICAL SIGNATURE...
...SO SET COURSE FOR THE CADAVEROUS CRYPTS, FLYNN.
RIGHTY-O, MAGS! YOU GUYS MADE THE RIGHT CALL BRINGING THE OL' FLYNNSTER.
BUT EVEN WITH WALLOP ALONG, ARE YOU SURE WE'VE GOT ENOUGH FIREPOWER FOR A MISSION OF THIS MAGNITUDE?
DON'T WORRY, LITTLE BUDDY...
...I'M ALL THE MUSCLE WE'LL NEED!
HEX? ARE YOU OKAY?
I'M FINE, SPYRO. PLEASE, GO BACK TO WHATEVER YOU WERE DOING.
LOOK, I KNOW SOME SKYLANDERS HAVE GIVEN YOU A HARD TIME IN THE PAST, BUT I'VE NEVER DOUBTED YOUR LOYALTIES.
WE'LL NEED TO WORK TOGETHER TO GET OUR POWERS BACK, AND STOP WHOEVER IS BEHIND THIS. YOU HAVE TO GIVE TRUST TO GET TRUST.
I KNOW, SPYRO. THERE'S JUST SOMETHING ABOUT THIS, ABOUT THE TWO OF US BEING TARGETED, THAT BRINGS UP OLD FEELINGS. FEELINGS I THOUGHT I WAS OVER.
I'M SORRY FOR BEING ABRASIVE, BUT THIS ENTIRE SITUATION MAKES ME SO UNEASY.
I DON'T KNOW IF THIS IS GOOD NEWS OR BAD NEWS, BUT YOU GUYS SHOULD COME SEE THIS.
BECAUSE NOW I'M GETTING TWO READINGS!

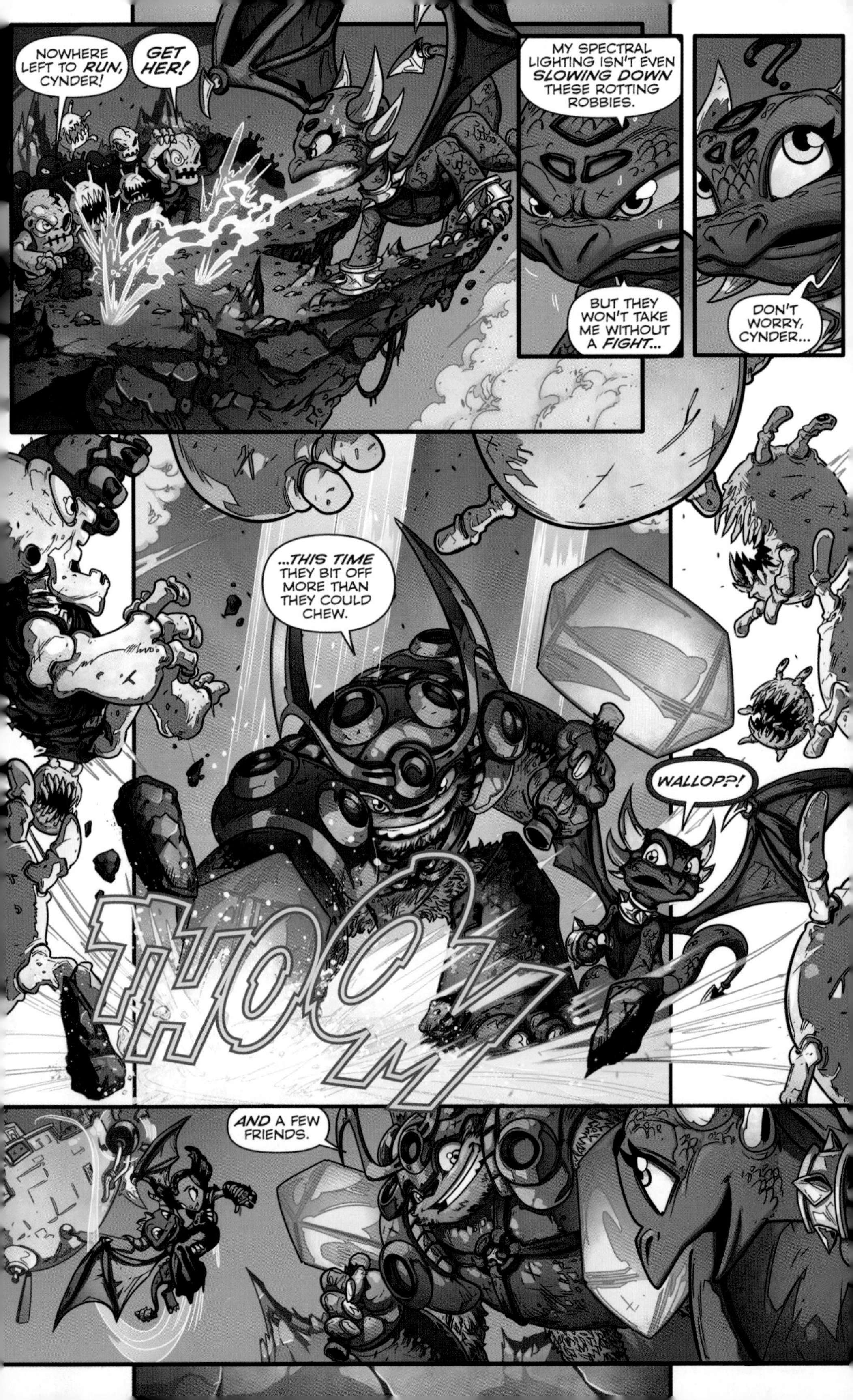
NOWHERE LEFT TO RUN, CYNDER!
GET HER!
MY SPECTRAL LIGHTING ISN'T EVEN SLOWING DOWN THESE ROTTING ROBBIES.
BUT THEY WON'T TAKE ME WITHOUT A FIGHT...
DON'T WORRY, CYNDER...
...THIS TIME THEY BIT OFF MORE THAN THEY COULD CHEW.
WALLOP?!
THOOM
AND A FEW FRIENDS.

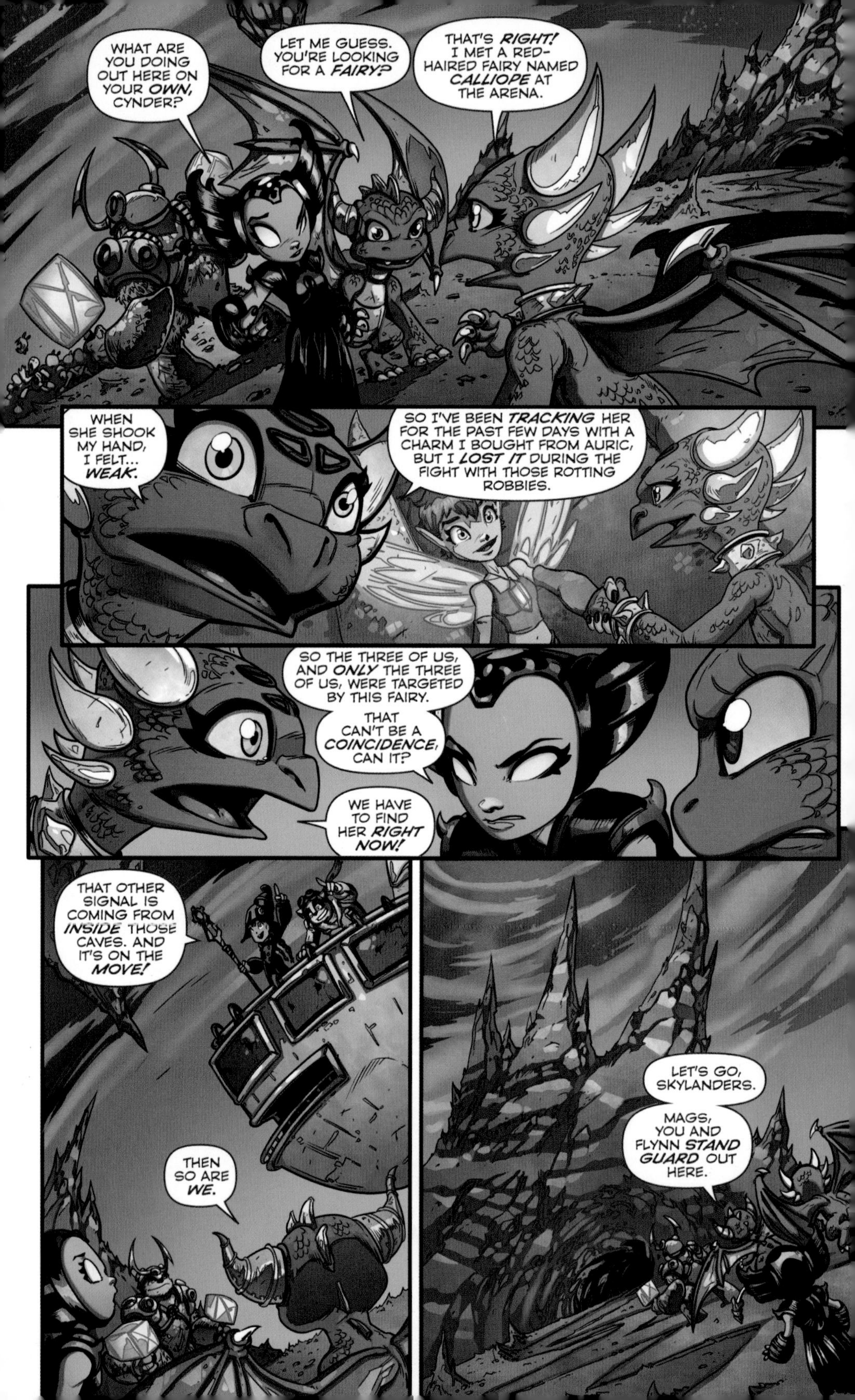
WHAT ARE YOU DOING OUT HERE ON YOUR OWN, CYNDER?
LET ME GUESS. YOU'RE LOOKING FOR A FAIRY?
THAT'S RIGHT! I MET A RED-HAIRED FAIRY NAMED CALLIOPE AT THE ARENA.
WHEN SHE SHOOK MY HAND, I FELT... WEAK.
SO I'VE BEEN TRACKING HER FOR THE PAST FEW DAYS WITH A CHARM I BOUGHT FROM AURIC, BUT I LOST IT DURING THE FIGHT WITH THOSE ROTTING ROBBIES.
SO THE THREE OF US, AND ONLY THE THREE OF US, WERE TARGETED BY THIS FAIRY.
THAT CAN'T BE A COINCIDENCE, CAN IT?
WE HAVE TO FIND HER RIGHT NOW!
THAT OTHER SIGNAL IS COMING FROM INSIDE THOSE CAVES. AND IT'S ON THE MOVE!
THEN SO ARE WE.
LET'S GO, SKYLANDERS.
MAGS, YOU AND FLYNN STAND GUARD OUT HERE.

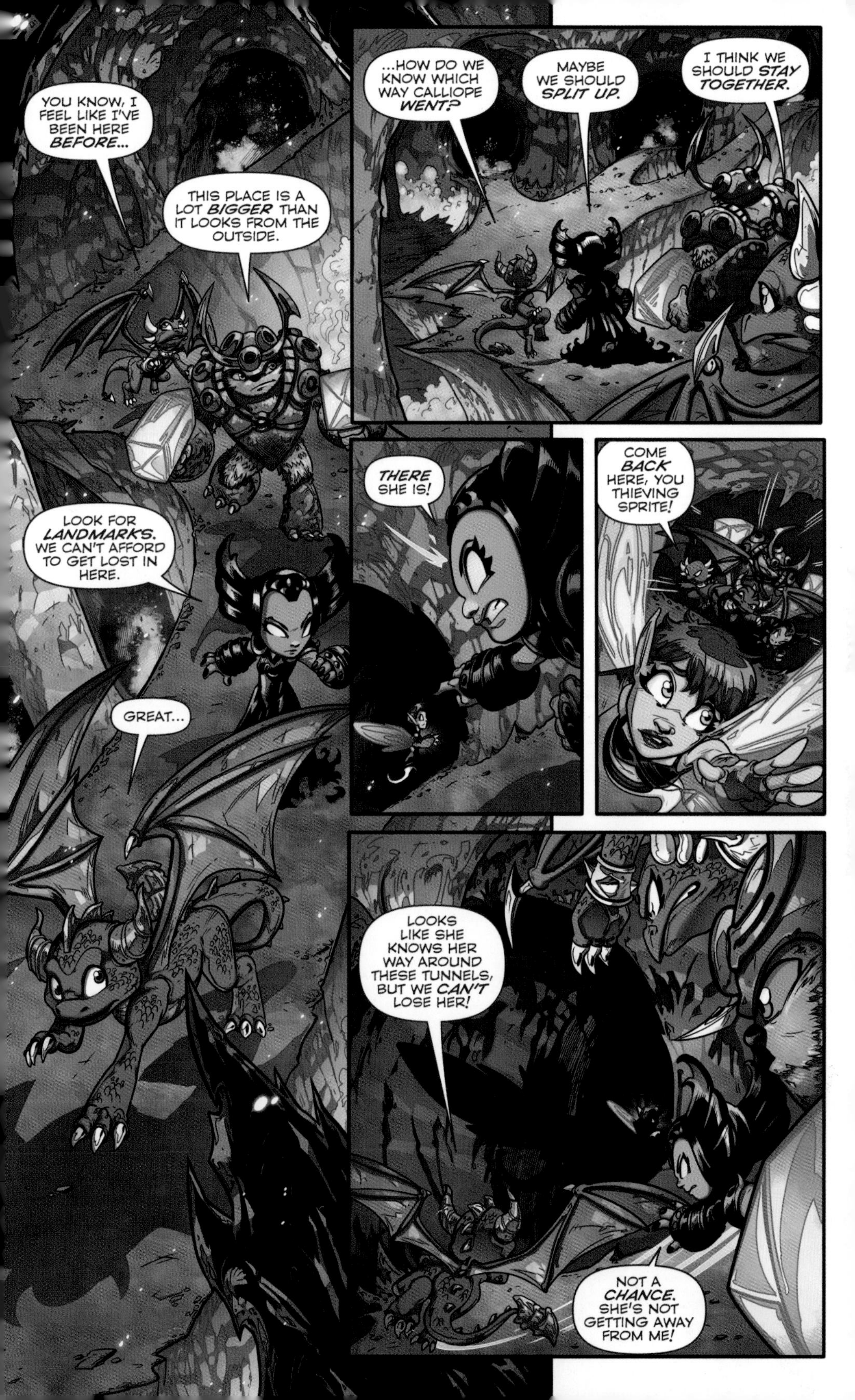
YOU KNOW, I FEEL LIKE I'VE BEEN HERE BEFORE...
THIS PLACE IS A LOT BIGGER THAN IT LOOKS FROM THE OUTSIDE.
LOOK FOR LANDMARKS. WE CAN'T AFFORD TO GET LOST IN HERE.
GREAT...
...HOW DO WE KNOW WHICH WAY CALLIOPE WENT?
MAYBE WE SHOULD SPLIT UP.
I THINK WE SHOULD STAY TOGETHER.
THERE SHE IS!
COME BACK HERE, YOU THIEVING SPRITE!
LOOKS LIKE SHE KNOWS HER WAY AROUND THESE TUNNELS, BUT WE CAN'T LOSE HER!
NOT A CHANCE. SHE'S NOT GETTING AWAY FROM ME!

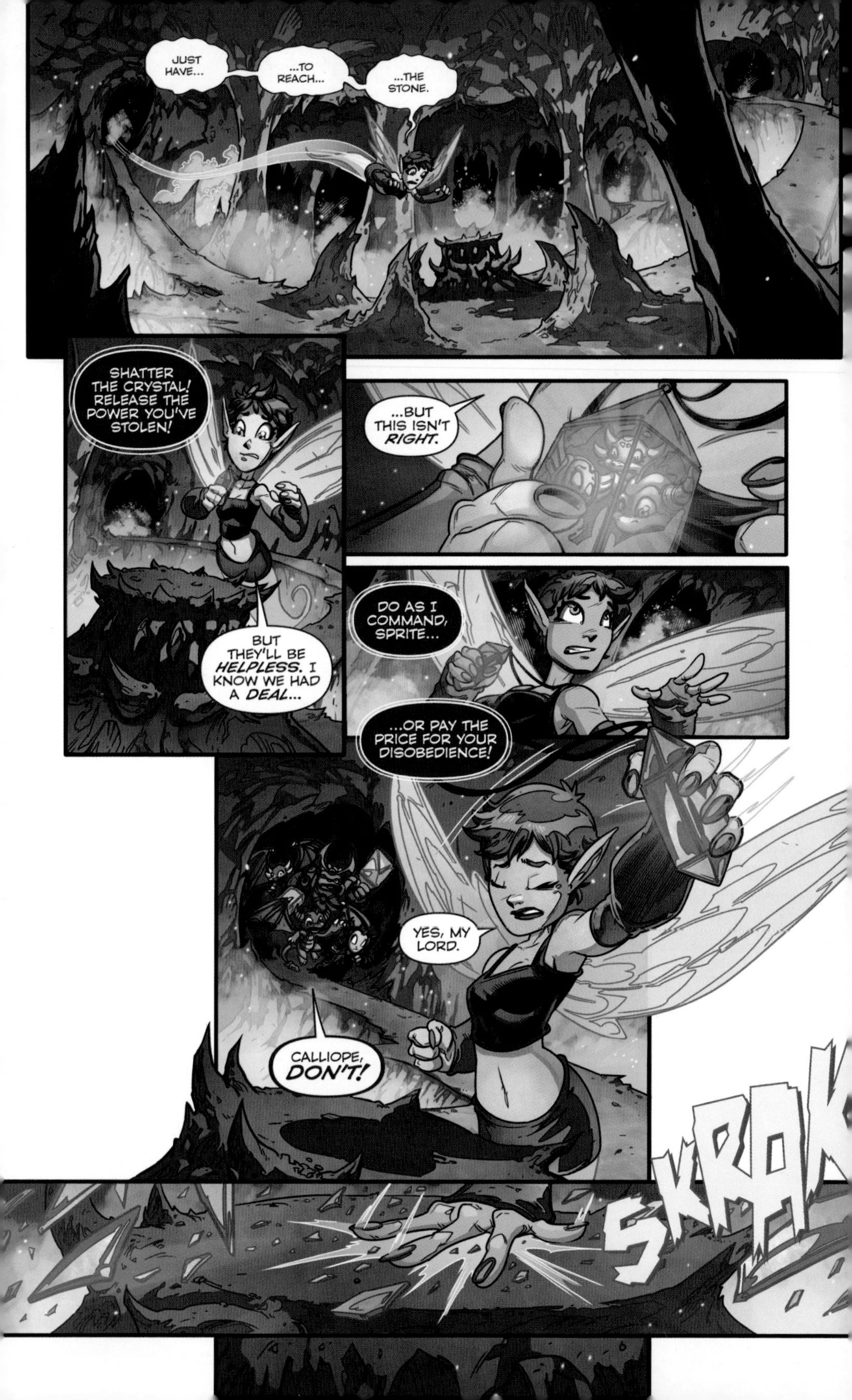
JUST HAVE...
...TO REACH...
...THE STONE.
SHATTER THE CRYSTAL! RELEASE THE POWER YOU'VE STOLEN!
...BUT THIS ISN'T RIGHT.
BUT THEY'LL BE HELPLESS. I KNOW WE HAD A DEAL...
DO AS I COMMAND, SPRITE...
...OR PAY THE PRICE FOR YOUR DISOBEDIENCE!
YES, MY LORD.
CALLIOPE, DON'T!
SKRAK

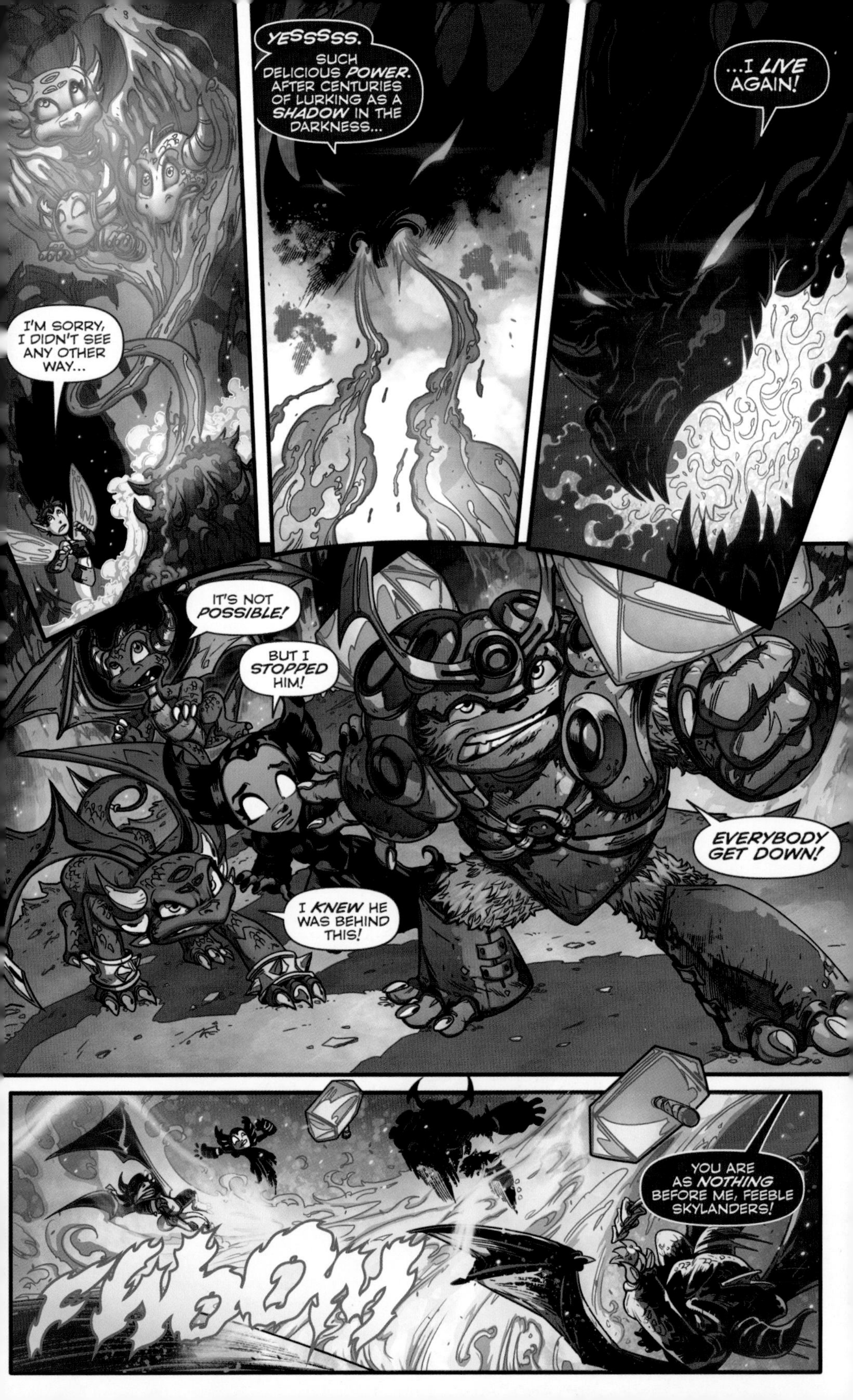
I'M SORRY, I DIDN'T SEE ANY OTHER WAY...
YESSSSS. SUCH DELICIOUS POWER. AFTER CENTURIES OF LURKING AS A SHADOW IN THE DARKNESS...
...I LIVE AGAIN!
IT'S NOT POSSIBLE!
BUT I STOPPED HIM!
EVERYBODY GET DOWN!
I KNEW HE WAS BEHIND THIS!
YOU ARE AS NOTHING BEFORE ME, FEEBLE SKYLANDERS!

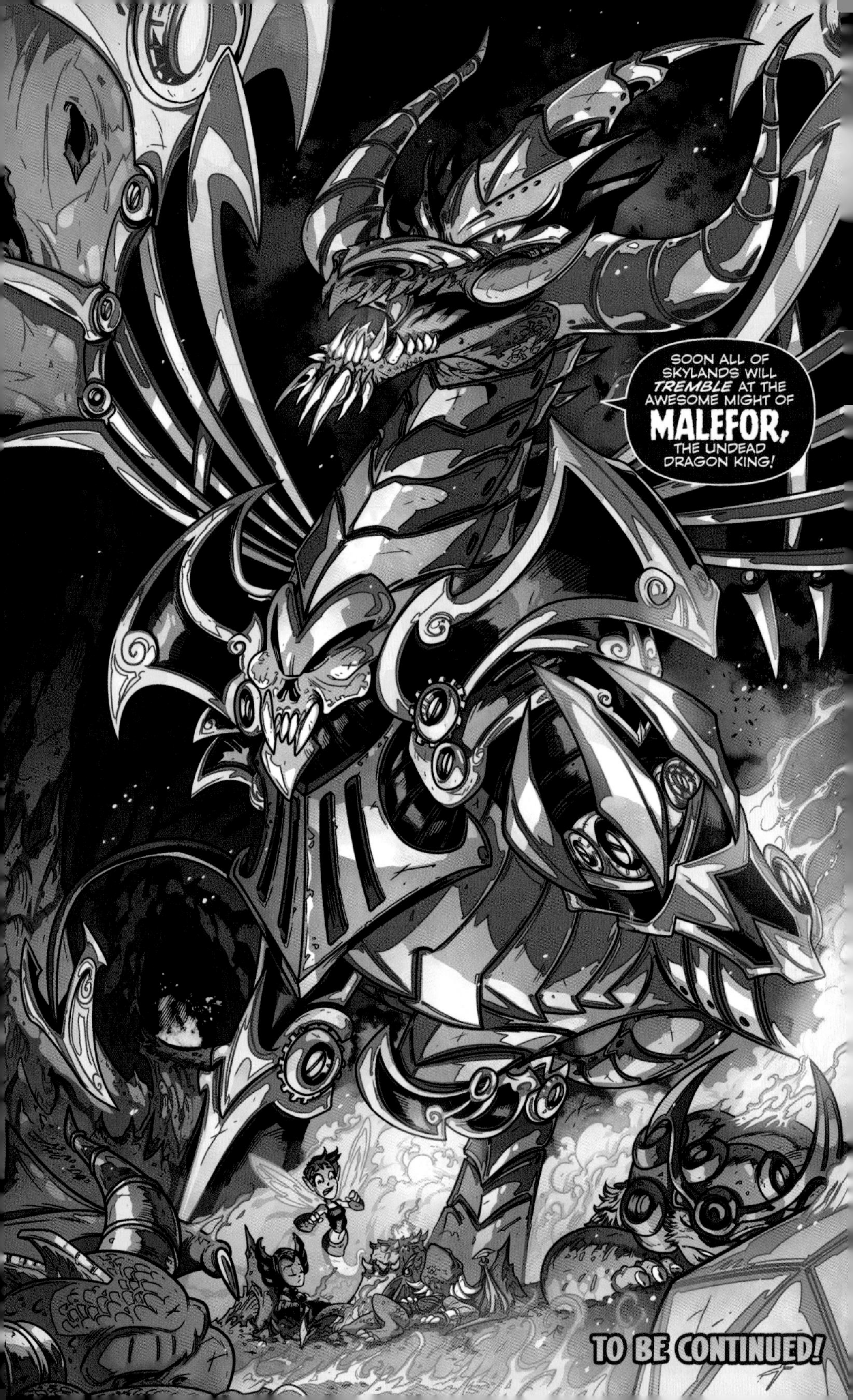
SOON ALL OF SKYLANDS WILL TREMBLE AT THE AWESOME MIGHT OF MALEFOR, THE UNDEAD DRAGON KING!
TO BE CONTINUED!

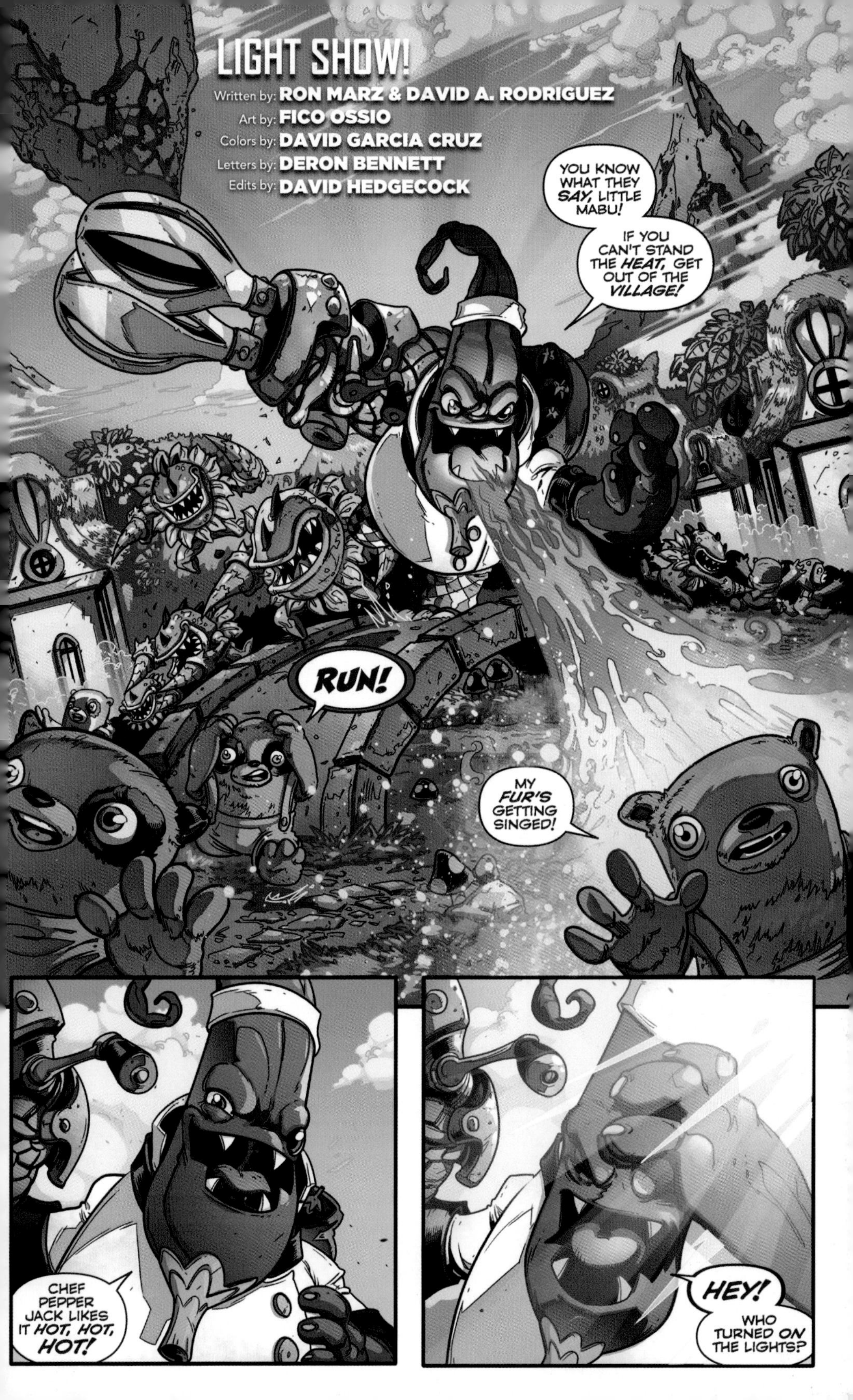
LIGHT SHOW!
Written by: RON MARZ & DAVID A. RODRIGUEZ
Art by: FICO OSSIO
Colors by: DAVID GARCIA CRUZ
Letters by: DERON BENNETT
Edits by: DAVID HEDGECOCK
YOU KNOW WHAT THEY SAY, LITTLE MABU!
IF YOU CAN'T STAND THE HEAT, GET OUT OF THE VILLAGE!
RUN!
MY FUR'S GETTING SINGED!
CHEF PEPPER JACK LIKES IT HOT, HOT, HOT!
HEY!
WHO TURNED ON THE LIGHTS?

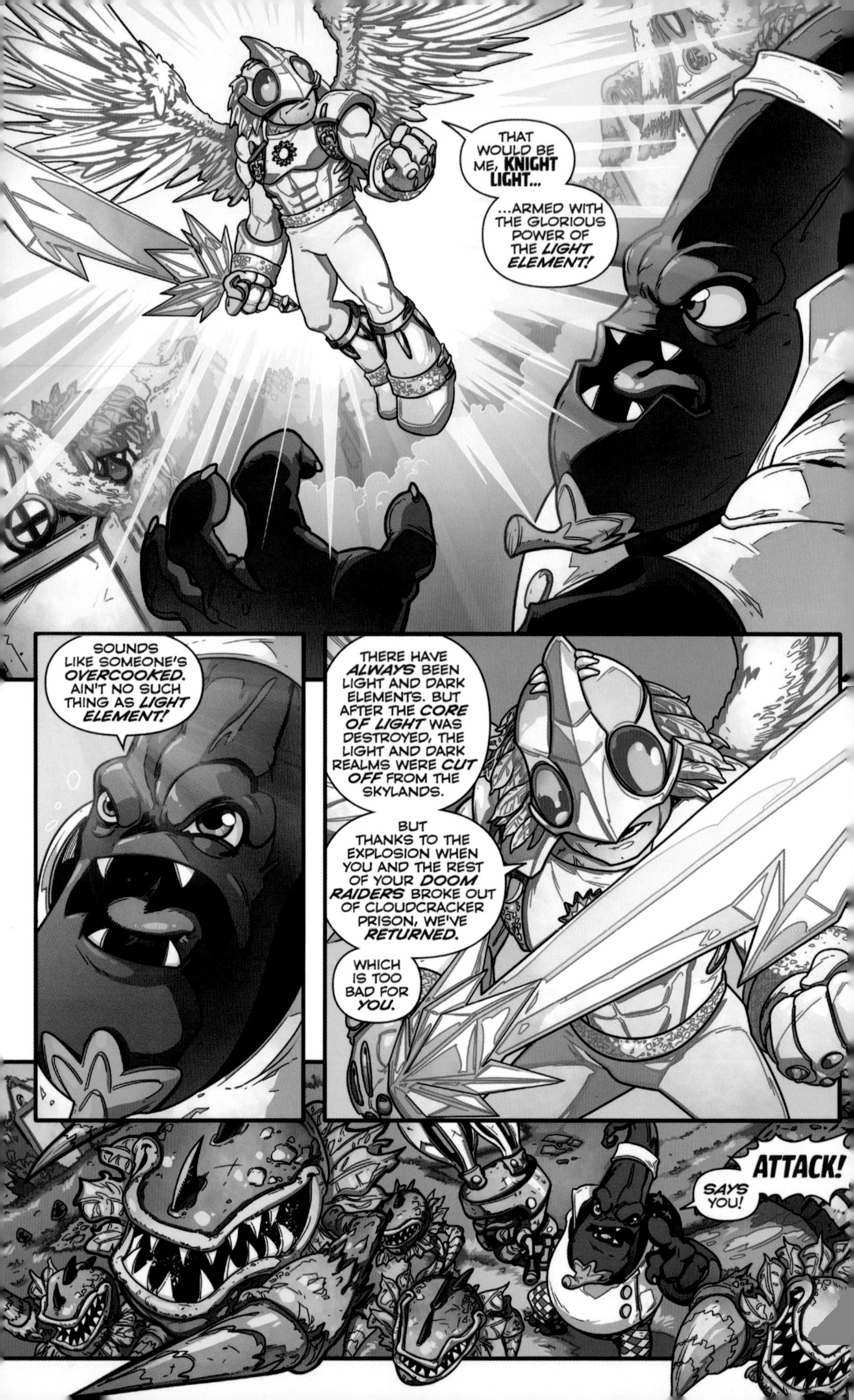

THAT WOULD BE ME, KNIGHT LIGHT...
...ARMED WITH THE GLORIOUS POWER OF THE LIGHT ELEMENT!
SOUNDS LIKE SOMEONE'S OVERCOOKED. AIN'T NO SUCH THING AS LIGHT ELEMENT!
THERE HAVE ALWAYS BEEN LIGHT AND DARK ELEMENTS. BUT AFTER THE CORE OF LIGHT WAS DESTROYED, THE LIGHT AND DARK REALMS WERE CUT OFF FROM THE SKYLANDS.
BUT THANKS TO THE EXPLOSION WHEN YOU AND THE REST OF YOUR DOOM RAIDERS BROKE OUT OF CLOUDCRACKER PRISON, WE'VE RETURNED.
WHICH IS TOO BAD FOR YOU.
SAYS YOU!
ATTACK!

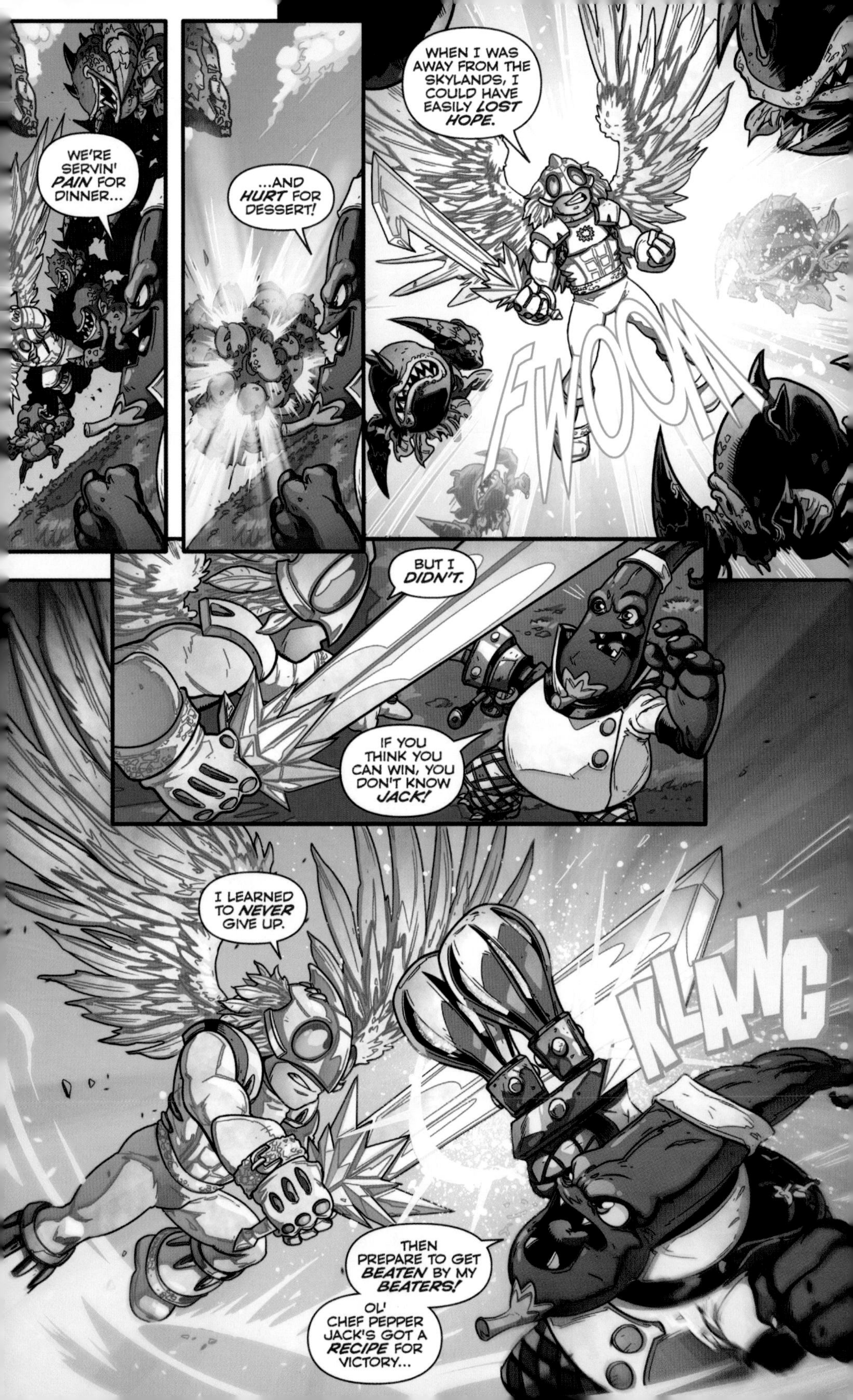
WE'RE SERVIN' *PAIN* FOR DINNER...
...AND *HURT* FOR DESSERT!
WHEN I WAS AWAY FROM THE SKYLANDS, I COULD HAVE EASILY *LOST HOPE.*
FWOOM
BUT I *DIDN'T.*
IF YOU THINK YOU CAN WIN, YOU DON'T KNOW *JACK!*
I LEARNED TO *NEVER* GIVE UP.
KLANG
THEN PREPARE TO GET *BEATEN* BY MY *BEATERS!*
OL' CHEF PEPPER JACK'S GOT A *RECIPE* FOR VICTORY...

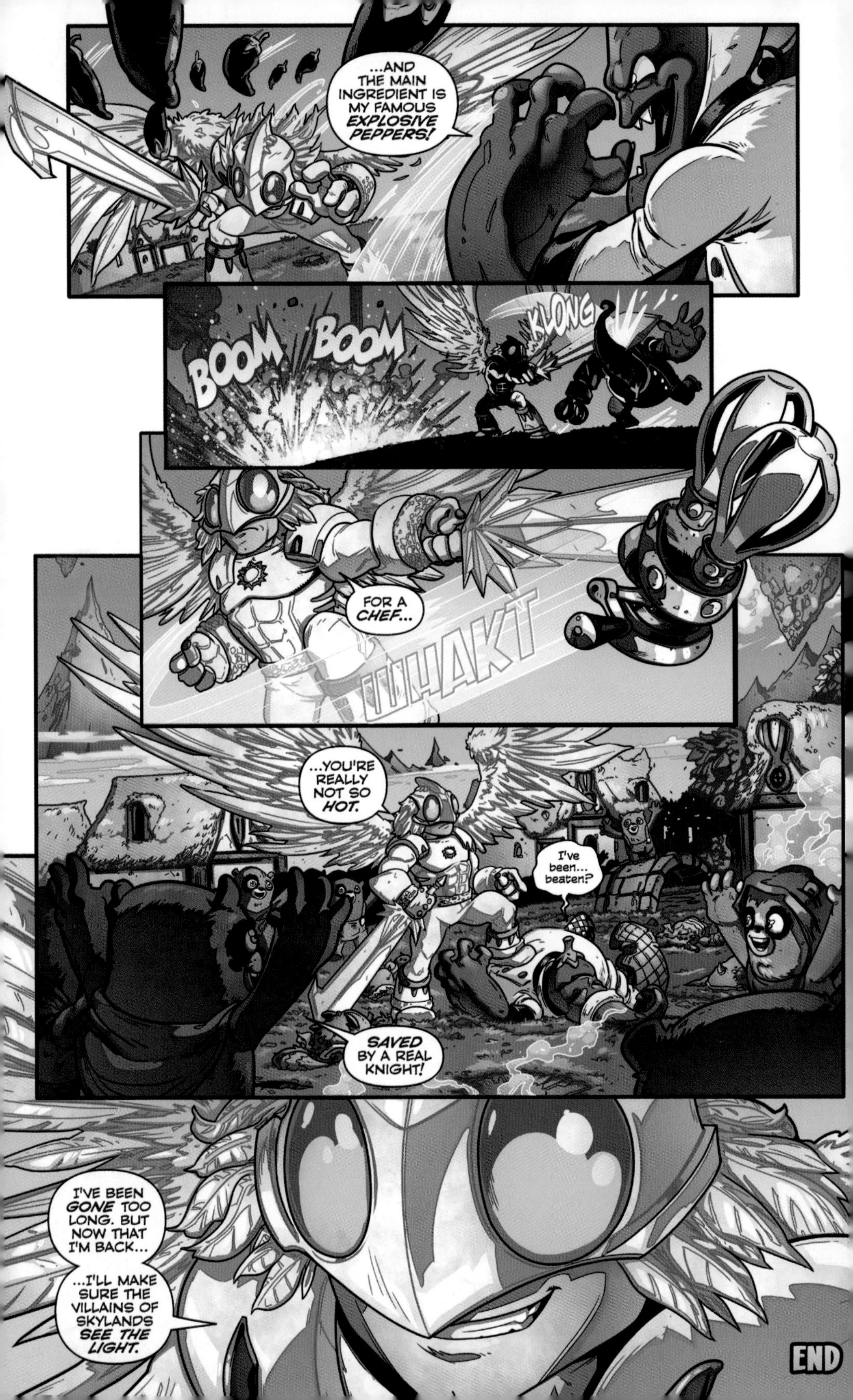
...AND THE MAIN INGREDIENT IS MY FAMOUS EXPLOSIVE PEPPERS!
BOOM
BOOM
KLONG
FOR A CHEF...
WHAKT
...YOU'RE REALLY NOT SO HOT.
I've been... beaten?
SAVED BY A REAL KNIGHT!
I'VE BEEN GONE TOO LONG. BUT NOW THAT I'M BACK...
...I'LL MAKE SURE THE VILLAINS OF SKYLANDS SEE THE LIGHT.
END

SKYLANDERS™

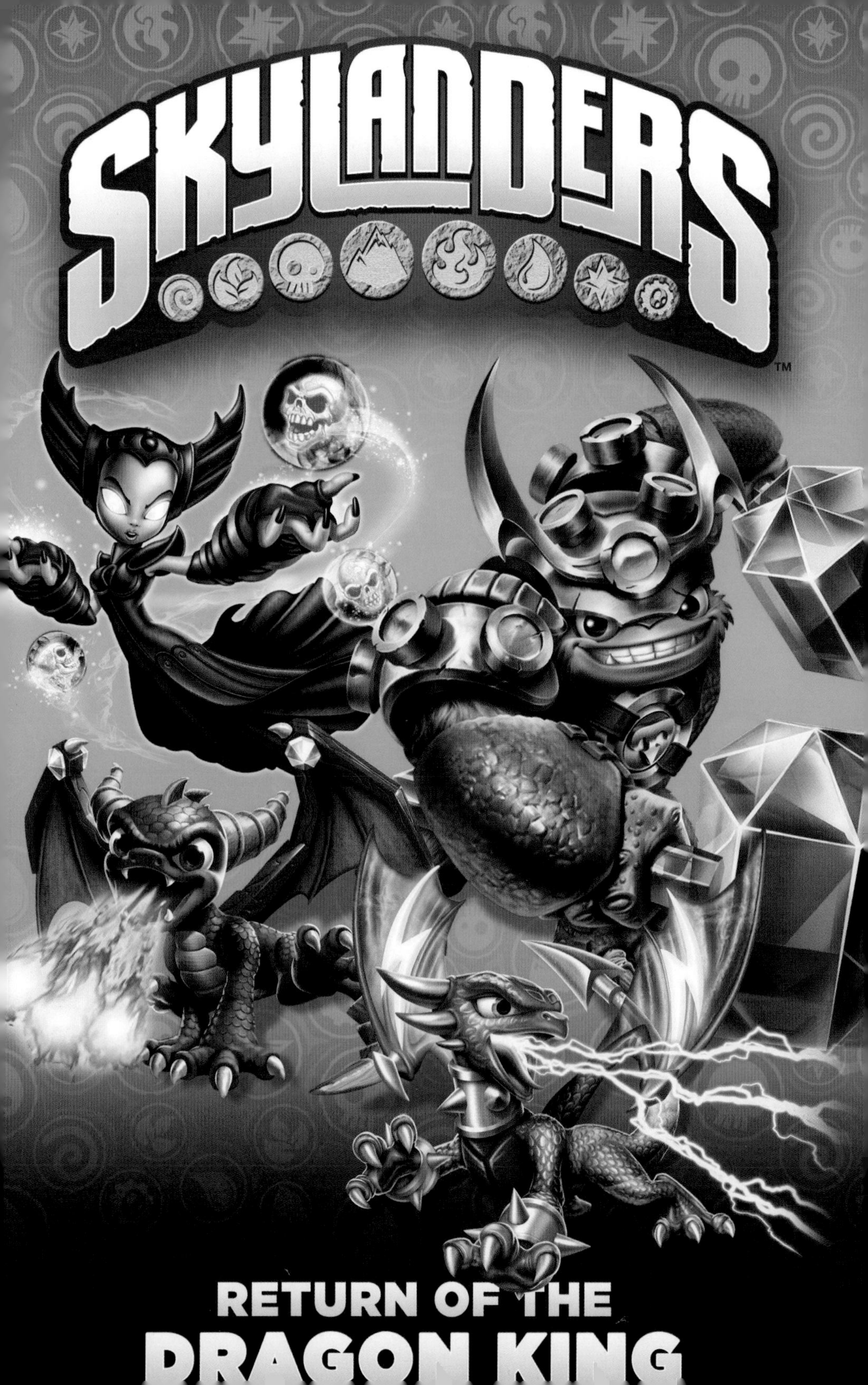

RETURN OF THE DRAGON KING

COLLECT THEM ALL!

Set of 6 Hardcover Books ISBN: 978-1-5321-4242-0

Hardcover Book ISBN
978-1-5321-4243-7

Hardcover Book ISBN
978-1-5321-4244-4

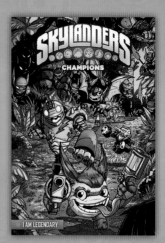

Hardcover Book ISBN
978-1-5321-4245-1

Hardcover Book ISBN
978-1-5321-4246-8

Hardcover Book ISBN
978-1-5321-4247-5

Hardcover Book ISBN
978-1-5321-4248-2